panda series

PANDA books are for first readers beginning to make their own way through books.

Granny's Secret

BRIANÓG BRADY DAWSON

• Pictures by Michael Connor •

THE O'BRIEN PRESS
DUBLIN

First published 2001 by The O'Brien Press Ltd.,
20 Victoria Road, Dublin 6, Ireland.
Tel: +353 1 4923333; Fax: +353 1 4922777
E-mail: books@obrien.ie
Website: www.obrien.ie.

ISBN: 0-86278-726-2

1   2   3   4   5   6   7   8   9   10
01   02   03   04   05   06   07   08   09   10

British Library Cataloguing-in-Publication Data
Dawson, Brianog Brady
Granny's secret. - (Pandas ; 21)
1.Children's stories
I.Title II.Connor, Michael
823.9'14[J]

The O'Brien Press receives
assistance from

**the arts
council**
an chomhairle
ealaíon
50

Typesetting, layout, editing: The O'Brien Press Ltd.
Cover separations: C&A Print Services Ltd.
Printing: Cox & Wyman Ltd.

For the Brady boys:
Eoghan, Cian, Ruairí and Oisín,
with love.

Can YOU spot the panda
hidden in the story?

Granny spoke to Danny
on the phone.

'You're all coming to stay
at my house,' she said.
'You, Susie, Mum and Dad.
For the whole weekend.'

'Great!' said Danny.

Danny looked
at his dog, Keeno.

'Can I bring Keeno
instead of Susie?' he asked.

Granny laughed.
'Oh Danny!' she said.
'Don't be mean.
Keeno can come too.'

'And,' said Granny,
'I have a **big secret**
to show you.'

When they got
to Granny's house
Danny was very excited.
'Show me your secret, Granny!'
he said.

Granny took Danny upstairs.
She went into the spare room.

'You will sleep here, Danny,'
she said. 'And this is where
I hid my **secret**.
You must look after it for me.'

Granny opened
the wardrobe door.
On a shelf was
a big birthday cake.

It had fluffy white icing
all over the top.
There were decorations
all around the edges.

And there were
four big pink candles
on the top.

Danny was puzzled.
'But, Granny,' he said,
'who's going to be four?
Not me. Not Susie.
Not Keeno.'

Granny smiled.

'It's for your mum,' she said.

'Tomorrow is her birthday.

But she mustn't see the cake.

It's my **surprise**.'

'But Mum's not four!'

said Danny.

Granny just smiled.

'You keep my secret, Danny,'

she said.

'I'll keep your secret, Granny,'
said Danny.
'I won't tell Mum.'

Granny gave Danny a hug.
'And you'll keep Keeno
out of this room,
won't you, dear?' she said.
'He can sleep outside.'

Danny was stunned.
Keep Keeno out of
my room! he thought.
No way!

But he smiled at Granny.
'Your secret is safe, Granny,'
he said sweetly.

When Granny left,
Danny thumped the bed.
'No! No! No!' he said.

'Keeno always sleeps
in my room.
Granny can't put him
outside.'

Then Danny had a great idea.
'I could find a hiding place
here for Keeno.'
He looked around the room.

First, Danny looked
under the bed.
He tried to crawl in.

But there wasn't much room.

Then he tried
the big wooden blanket box.

But that was
very dark and stuffy.

Then he opened the wardrobe.
There was plenty of room
for a dog in there.
There was even
a nice smell.

'This is a great hiding place,'
said Danny.
'I'll put Keeno in here!'

Danny looked at
Granny's secret.
He was worried.
'If Keeno eats
Granny's secret,' he said,
'I'll be in big trouble!'

'I know what I'll do!'
cried Danny suddenly.
'I'll find another hiding place
for Granny's secret!
Then Keeno can hide
in the wardrobe!'

Danny lifted the cake
out of the wardrobe.

'This is not very big,'
he said to himself.
'This will fit
under the bed.'

Danny put the cake
on the floor.
He slid it under the bed.
But the candles fell off.

'Those candles were **stupid**,
anyway,' said Danny.
'Mum is much older
than four.'

Suddenly Mum came
into the bedroom.
She was carrying
her weekend bag.
She walked over to the bed.
She put the bag on the floor.

'At last,' she said,
'I've finished unpacking.'

Mum kicked the bag
under the bed!
Then she left the room.

Danny was speechless.

'Oh no!' said Danny.
'Mum has **ruined**
Granny's secret.'

He crawled under the bed.

He pulled the bag out.

He reached for Granny's secret
and dragged it out.

There was an old shoe
stuck in the lovely icing.

Danny was very cross
with Mum.
'It's her own fault
if she gets no surprise!'
he said.
'Mum should be
more careful!'

Danny decided to find
a better hiding place
for Granny's secret.
He lifted the lid
of the big wooden blanket box.

Very carefully,
Danny put Granny's secret
on top of the blankets.
He closed the lid.

'Now,' said Danny,
'Granny's secret is safe.'
He raced downstairs
to get Keeno.

Danny sneaked Keeno
up to the bedroom.
He found Susie
sitting on the floor,
playing with her bricks.

'Out of my way, Susie!'
said Danny.
'I have to hide Keeno.'

Danny pushed past his sister.
He opened the wardrobe door.
He put Keeno in.

'Time for bed,' yelled Dad.

He came into the bedroom.

He tripped on a brick.

He hurt his foot.

'What a mess, Susie!'
said Dad.
He picked up Susie's bricks.
He lifted the lid
of the blanket box.
He threw the bricks in.
He carried Susie downstairs.

Danny was shocked.
He lifted the lid quickly
and peeped inside.
Two of Susie's bricks
were stuck in
Mum's birthday cake.

Danny fell back on the floor.
'Dad!' he groaned crossly,
'you've **ruined**
Granny's secret!'

'Granny's secret isn't safe
in this room,' said Danny.

'I'll have to find
somewhere else for it.'

Suddenly he had
a great idea.
'The shed!' he said.
'I'll hide Granny's secret
in the shed!
Mum will never find it there!'

Later, when everyone sat down
to watch television,
Danny crept downstairs
with Granny's secret.
He took it out to the shed.

Danny put Granny's secret
in the corner of the shed.
'Granny's secret
is safe at last!' he said.
'And Keeno is safe too.'

Danny ran upstairs
and got into bed.

Soon Granny came
into the room with Susie.
She put Susie in the cot.
A strange noise
came from the wardrobe.

Granny jumped.

'What was that?' she said.

'It was Susie!' cried Danny.
'She burped!'

Granny laughed and
gave Danny another
goodnight kiss.

As soon as Granny
left the room,
Danny jumped out of bed.
He opened the wardrobe door.
'It's safe, Keeno!' he cried.
'You can come out now.'

'Woof! Woof!'
barked Keeno happily.

But Granny came back
into the room.

'**Out**!' she yelled.
She marched Keeno
down the stairs.

Next day, everyone sang
'Happy Birthday' to Mum.

Granny got her camera ready.
'Now you must blow out
your candles,' she said.

Mum looked puzzled.
'But I don't have any candles,'
she said.

'We don't even have a cake!'
laughed Dad.

Granny winked at Danny.
'We have a **secret**,
don't we, Danny?' she said.
'Let's go and get it.'

Granny started to go upstairs.
'No, Granny!'
whispered Danny.
'Your secret wasn't safe there.
I put it in the shed.'

'In the shed!' cried Granny.
'But that's where I put Keeno!'

Granny ran out to the shed.

Danny shut his eyes tightly.

I hope Keeno doesn't like icing,
he thought.

Soon Granny marched
out of the shed again.
Her face was purple.
She was dragging Keeno
with one hand.

And she was holding
Mum's birthday cake
in the other hand.

Danny opened his eyes.
'**Oh no**!' he said.
He looked at the cake.

The candles were gone.

There was an old shoe
sitting on the top.

Two of Susie's bricks
were stuck in the icing.

And Keeno had eaten
a big hole in the cake!

'**Danny**!' yelled Granny.
'You've ruined my secret!'

Danny ran.
'It's Mum's fault!
It's Dad's fault!
It's Keeno's fault!'
he squealed.

He ran all around the garden.

Granny ran after him –
and Mum,
and Dad,
and Keeno.

'I'll never do anything
like this again,' Danny yelled.
'Never. Never. Never.'

But I think he will, don't you?
Danny's just that kind of kid!